3 414489 21

First published in 2000
This edition re-issued in 2011

Wayland
338 Euston Road
London NW1 3BH

Wayland Australia
Level 17/207 Kent Street
Sydney, NSW 2000

British Library Cataloguing in Publication Data available

ISBN 978 0 7502 6560  7

Printed in China

Wayland is a division of Hachette Children's Books,
an Hachette UK company

# TESSA POTTER

# THE SPECTRE IN SCHOOL LANE

*Illustrated by Andrew Skilleter*

WAYLAND

341448921

# Chapter One

It was an ordinary sort of morning, I was late as usual. I'd just turned into the Avenue when I heard him – well *sensed* him really. I just knew that there was something there behind me. I stopped and turned.

For a second I could hardly breathe.
A huge, thin, grey dog was coming towards
me. I stared in horror. It was him! It was
old Grey-Hair! I wanted the pavement to
swallow me up.

I tried to look away. I didn't want him to
see I was scared. And I knew I mustn't run,
not this time. I knew what happened if you
ran. If you ran Grey-Hair would get you.

He seemed to be staring straight at me with angry, accusing, dark eyes. Closer and closer he came. I could feel my heart pounding.

Then suddenly it was over.

He trotted quietly past me and on down the pavement. With a final glance, he crossed the road and disappeared down School Lane.

I almost laughed out loud with relief.

Then I began to feel weird. I was shaking. Grey-Hair? How could it have been Grey-Hair? Grey-Hair was dead. If anyone knew that, I did. I'd seen him lying under the car wheels. I'd seen his shattered head against the kerb, his staring eyes. And I'd done it. They all said it was my fault. If I hadn't run, he wouldn't have chased me and the car wouldn't have got him.

I stood still for a moment staring down at the pavement. It had been four years since Grey-Hair's accident. I'd tried to block it out, tried to forget it. Although I had to pass the same spot every day, I hadn't thought about him. But suddenly, now, it had all come flooding back…

# Chapter Two

*I'd been in the Infants in those days, in Mrs Small's class. I wasn't the only one who was scared of him – we all were. Old Grey-Hair was always there. Every Tuesday on the way to swimming he'd be lying on the pavement, waiting for us, his grey head resting on huge paws, his red, bloodshot eyes staring up at us.*

*Sam's brother told us how he would come up behind you, grab your swimming bag, toss it in the air and shake it like a rat.*

And how he'd knocked over Sarah Biggs.

"Don't ever walk at the end of the line," he told us. "You're all right in the middle. It's the people at the end he gets. And you have to walk slowly past him, don't run. If he thinks you're scared, he'll get you."

*The day Grey-Hair had died had been a cold autumn day, just like today.*

*"Line up quietly near the gate, children," Miss Small said.*

*But Sam and I charged. We wanted a good place, not too near the front with Miss and definitely not at the back! We bumped into Tracy by mistake and she fell over. Miss Small said we were pushing.*

"You two can go right to the back," she said.

I remember my heart sinking, the feeling in my stomach. "But, Miss!" I stammered. "We… we didn't do anything."

"To the back, Roy Chapman!" said Miss Small, sternly.

Sam and I looked at each other. We took our places slowly at the end of the line. Perhaps we'd be lucky, perhaps Grey-Hair wouldn't be there today.

But Grey-Hair was there. We knew as soon as we crossed School Lane and turned into the Avenue. Everything at the front suddenly went quiet. The quiet spread down the line. Everybody slowed down and stopped kicking the leaves and swinging their bags.

"Hurry up, you lot," shrieked Miss Small. "Don't dawdle. We'll never get there. Take no notice of the dog and he'll leave you alone."

I think Miss Small's shrill voice wound Grey-Hair up. By the time we reached him, he wasn't lying down any more. He was standing up and growling softly.

We were level with him now. Sam was on the outside by the road. I was on the inside right next to him. I thought I was going to die. I tried not to look scared. I clutched my swimming bag and hugged it tightly to my chest.

"I think we're all right now," Sam whispered to me. Then he gulped. "Oh no, he's following us."

I glanced round. I saw the gleam in old Grey-Hair's eyes. I saw the slobber on his jaws. I saw his lolling tongue. And I saw his long yellow teeth. Then suddenly he dived, straight for me.

I had to run. What else could I have done? Perhaps I should have dropped the bag, perhaps it was just the bag he wanted, not me. I only wanted to get away. I ran across the road and Grey-Hair tore after me.

*I remember Miss Small's scream and the
thud as the car hit him. I remember people
crying and Grey-Hair lying there in the road.*

*Then everything went blank. They said I
had shock. My mum came and took me home.*

# Chapter Three

...So that had been it, the end of poor Grey-
Hair. How long had I been standing there
remembering? I stared at my watch. I'd have
to run now if I was going to get to school in
time. I crossed into School Lane, praying
that the dog would have gone. There was
no sign of him. He seemed to have vanished.
Sam was waiting for me by the school gates.

"Come on, you're late."

"Did you see him?" I began. "The dog... he was just like Grey-Hair"

But Sam wasn't listening. "Bad news," he panted as we ran across the playground. "Morgan's away today."

Mr Morgan was the best teacher we had. We all liked him.

"I wonder who we'll get," Sam groaned.

As we ran up the steps we nearly knocked over Mrs Price, the Headteacher.

"Slow down, you two," she said.

There was a tall man with her. He wore a dark suit. His hair was grey and he had a thin white moustache.

"I think these are two of yours, Mr Stringer," Mrs Price told him, smiling. "Keen, aren't they?"

The man nodded. He said nothing, but his top lip curled into a smile. He looked at us. His eyes seemed to go through me.

I shuddered.

"Get to your class, please, boys," said Mrs Price. "We'll be along in a minute."

Mr Stringer seemed to have it in for me right from the start. It was strange how he knew my name. Normally new teachers don't remember your name straight away.

"Roy Chapman," he called. "Give out these books, please."

Thirty-five comprehension books, that would take forever.

"On my own, sir?" I asked.

"Not strong enough?" he snarled. "Get on with it, please."

As I tried to lift up the pile, the top ones slid to the floor and when I bent down to pick them up, the rest slipped out of my arms.

"Butter-fingers!" he hissed, baring long yellow teeth.

I heard a few titters. My face went red.

Mr Stringer sneered. "Somebody had better help the poor boy."

Sam was quickly by my side and we gave out the books together.

"He's *awful*!" whispered Sam.

Mr Stringer kept us doing comprehension exercises all morning. My biro ran out and I had to get another one from the bottom of my bag, which meant tipping out everything on to my desk – lunch box, games kit and my new comic.

Stringer came over. "What are you doing?"
he asked.

"Looking for another biro, sir," I told him.

He picked up the comic. "I'll take that,"
he said.

"But you can't," I blurted out. "It's mine."

"You shouldn't be reading it now," he
snarled. "You can get it from me at the end
of school."

"It's not fair, I wasn't reading it," I said,
trying to explain. But he wouldn't listen. He
said I was answering back. He made me sit
at the front, right next to his desk, for the
rest of the day. I felt sick and miserable.
I hated him.

At the end of school Sam and I raced to the staffroom. I was determined to get my comic back.

"Sorry, boys, Mr Stringer's just left," Mrs Price said.

"Come on," I yelled to Sam. "We'll catch up with him."

As we ran down the front steps I caught sight of a tall, dark figure disappearing out of the gates. "There he is," I shouted.

We tore after him, out of the gates and into School Lane. But it was completely deserted. We looked at each other.

"Where's he gone?" said Sam. "He can't have reached the Avenue yet."

As I stared down the empty lane, my heart stopped. There, among the swirling leaves, was the dog I'd seen that morning. Mr Stringer had vanished, but Grey-Hair had suddenly appeared. He was standing there very still, looking straight at us.

# Chapter Four

Sam didn't believe me about Grey-Hair.

"Don't be stupid!" he said. "Grey-Hair's dead! There's no such thing as ghost dogs. Stop trying to wind me up. It's just a stray that looks like Grey-Hair." But he did think it was a bit weird the way Mr Stringer had vanished.

I didn't put the two together, not at first, not until that night. I know it was only a dream, but it made me realize the truth, made me understand what was really happening. It was the most awful dream I'd ever had.

I was running down the road. Mr Stringer was following me, waving my comic.

However fast I ran, he was always just behind me. I ran and ran, but I couldn't get any further away from him. I kept glancing back, praying he'd be gone, but he was always just as close, even though he was only walking. I could see the slight curl on his lip, the yellow teeth, his red, staring eyes.

And then suddenly it wasn't Mr Stringer
at all. It was Grey-hair. It was Grey-Hair
coming down the road after me! I could hear
him panting, feel his hot breath on my legs.

I tried to scream, but no scream came out. I tore on down the road, desperate to get away. I glanced back again. Grey-Hair had gone. It was Stringer now. I kept turning my head backwards and forwards. Stringer, Grey-Hair. Grey-Hair, Stringer. They kept changing, like those pictures you spin until they merge into one. And then I realized – Stringer, Grey-Hair – they were the same.

I don't remember anything after that, except waking up. My heart was pounding. I lay there until the morning, staring into the darkness, too scared to close my eyes, wondering how I could ever go into school again. Grey-Hair had returned to take his revenge. He'd come back to make my life as miserable as possible. He'd come

back in the shape of Mr Stringer. That was why Stringer seemed to have it in for me. Mr Stringer was Grey-Hair! I started to feel horribly sick.

I stayed in bed all weekend. On Monday, Mum said I ought to go to school, because I didn't have a temperature or anything. As I walked into the gates, I prayed that Mr Morgan would be back, but he wasn't. Mr Stringer was still there.

We had PE first. I got changed in a daze, wondering what Stringer, Grey-Hair, had in store for me next.

All the apparatus had been arranged round the hall like an obstacle course. We had to line up and go round in turn, two circuits each. Stringer was timing us with a stop-watch. I heard my name.

"Roy Chapman. Go!"

I set off. My legs felt like lead. I managed the first horse. It was the bars next. My hands were sweating.

"Hurry up, Chapman. Is that the best you can do?"

I struggled on. Somehow I got round once. Stringer was in front of me now, the stop-watch in his hands.

"Terrible!" he sneered. "A six-year-old could go faster. Put some effort into it, Chapman. You're not trying."

"I feel sick," I mumbled trying to get my breath, but he took no notice.

"Again," he shouted, "and this time I'm coming after you. Let's see how you do now. You've got a start of five."

I set off again. I could hear him counting, chanting. Everyone was joining in. He was coming after me now, closer and closer. I reached the bars. I struggled up. I was near the top. My hands were slipping. I glanced down. I could see his face, the snarl on his lips. And then suddenly I wasn't scared any more. I just felt angry, really, *really* angry.

Why was he doing this to me? I hadn't meant to do anything. It hadn't been my fault. I hadn't meant to kill Grey-Hair.

"Leave me alone," I screamed. "I'm not afraid of you!" Then everything began to spin.

# Chapter Five

They weren't sure whether I'd hit my head or not when I fell. I remember everyone crowding round, and being taken to Mrs Price's office. I remember trying to explain to Mrs Price, trying to tell her about Mr Stringer being Grey-Hair's ghost.

"It's all right, Roy, dear," she said. "You've just had a bit of a fall. We've sent for your mum. She'll be here soon."

Then the phone went and Mrs Price had to leave me on my own. She said something had happened. It was playtime. I heard the bell go and everyone playing outside, then I remember the sound of a siren wailing.

I hoped my mum wouldn't be long.
I wanted to go home. I wanted to be
a million miles away from Mr Stringer.

I didn't hear the office door open,
but I knew he was there.

I knew it was him by the way the hairs on my neck stood up and everything went cold. I turned. Stringer was standing in front of me. He didn't say anything. He didn't snarl or sneer or curl his lip this time. His eyes looked different, not angry or staring any more. I knew then that it was over, that he wasn't coming back. "It wasn't my fault," I whispered. He seemed to nod and then he was gone.

Mrs Price looked very worried when she came in later with my mum. "I'm sorry to have left you alone so long, dear," she said.

When I told her I hadn't been alone, that Mr Stringer had come in, she went very white and had to sit down. Then she said that he couldn't have, that I must have been mistaken.

My mum told me later what had happened. There'd been an accident just before break. Mr Stringer had been crossing from School Lane into the Avenue. He'd walked straight into a car. There was nothing anyone could do...

As I listened to my mum a shiver ran through me. Mr Stringer had come into the office during breaktime. I was certain of that. He'd stood right in front of me. But how could he, if he was already dead?

I felt sick and strange. There was only one answer. It proved why Stringer had had it in for me all along. He really was a ghost – Grey-Hair's ghost. *Wasn't he...?*

# DARE TO BE SCARED!

*Are you brave enough to try more titles in the Tremors series? They're guaranteed to chill your spine...*

**Beware the Wicked Web** by Anthony Masters
In the dead of night, Rob and Sam explore the forbidden attic at the top of their new home. When they find a sprawling, sticky web, with a giant egg at its centre, they are scared – but not nearly as scared as when they discover that the egg is just about to hatch...

**The Headmaster's Ghost** by Sam Godwin
Danny's school trip would be great if he wasn't being bullied by Adam and Melissa. They try to scare him senseless with stories of the evil headmaster's ghost who is said to haunt the building. Then one dark night, Danny accepts Adam's dare to prove that he's not scared, but it brings more than he bargained for...

**The Root of Evil** by Barbara Mitchelhill
When Jake, Amy and Wez find the old pocket watch, they are thrilled. "We'll sell it!" says Jake. After all, finders are keepers, aren't they? So they sell the watch and go on a wild spending spree. But then things go horribly and frighteningly wrong...

*All these books and many more can be purchased from your local bookseller. For more information about Tremors, write to: The Sales Department, Hachette Children's Books, 338 Euston Road, London NW1 3BH.*